WALT DISNEY PRODUCTIONS
presents

Grandma Duck's Little Helpers

Random House New York

Donald Duck was going on a trip.
His nephews Huey, Louie, and Dewey
were going to stay with Grandma Duck
while Donald was away.
Donald told them what to do
to get ready.

Huey, Louie, and
Dewey packed up
the car.

They took their
toys and games.

They took their
balls and bats.

And they took
their fishing rods
and picnic basket.

Then Uncle Donald drove Huey, Louie, and
Dewey to Grandma Duck's farm in the country.
    The boys were so happy.
    They could not wait to get there.
    "We will have so much fun playing," they said.
    "Don't forget," said Donald, "you are here
to help Grandma, too."

Grandma Duck met them on the porch.
"Here are your little helpers, Grandma,"
said Donald. "I am sure they will get
a lot done."

"Of course," said Grandma
with a smile.
Then the four waved
good-bye to Donald as
he drove off.

First the boys unpacked
their things.

Huey hung up his coat
and hat.

Louie unpacked
his bag.

And Dewey took out
his bat and ball and
his other toys.

At the dinner table, Grandma said,
"Tomorrow will be a busy day. I am going
to plant some wheat, so we must all go
to bed early."

The next morning
Huey, Louie, and Dewey
ran to the barn to get
the gardening tools
Grandma wanted.

They were all ready
to help her plant
the wheat.

But when they went in the barn,
they found a bicycle with three seats.

They climbed up on the bales of
hay and took down the bicycle.

"Let's ride it," they said.

They forgot all
about the
planting.

The boys took the bicycle
out of the barn.

Grandma Duck saw them.
"Are you ready to help me
plant the wheat?" she asked.

"In a little while," said Huey, Louie,
and Dewey. "We want to try your bicycle
first. We will be right back!"

Then they waved and rode away.

"Well!" said Grandma Duck. "I guess
I will have to plant the wheat myself."

So she took her hoe and made
neat rows in the earth.

Then she planted the grains
of wheat one by one.

Finally she raked the loose
earth over the grains of wheat.

Grandma Duck was very tired
when she finished raking.

She heard a sound on the road
and looked up.

It was
Huey, Louie,
and Dewey
returning from
their ride.
"We are ready to help
you now, Grandma,"
they called.

Grandma was angry.
"You are too late," she said.
"I have planted the wheat myself."
"Oh, we're sorry, Grandma,"
said the boys.

The summer passed quickly,
and the wheat grew tall.
It was ready to be cut.
"I will ask the boys to help,"
said Grandma.

She found Huey, Louie, and
Dewey in the backyard.

They were digging up worms.

"Will you boys help me cut
the wheat?" she asked.
"Yes," they said.
"But we are going fishing
now. We will help you
when we get back.
We won't be long."

"Well!" said Grandma Duck.
"I guess I will have to cut
the wheat myself."

So she cut down all the stalks.

She gathered the
stalks together.

And she tied them into bunches.

Grandma Duck worked all day.
When she finished,
she was very tired.
She looked up to see Huey,
Louie, and Dewey.

They were each carrying
a fishing rod and a fish.
"Hi, Grandma," said Dewey.

"We brought you some fish
for dinner," said Huey.
"And we are ready to help
you with the wheat," said Louie.

"Thank you," said Grandma Duck,
"but you are too late. I have cut the
wheat myself. I could not wait all day
for you."

"Oh, we're sorry, Grandma," said
Huey, Louie, and Dewey. "It will not
happen again."

Soon the grain was dry.
It was ready to be taken
to the mill.

"I could use some help
from the boys today,"
said Grandma Duck.

She found Huey, Louie, and Dewey
in their bathing suits.

They were getting ready
to go to the beach.

"Will you help me take
the wheat to the mill?"
she asked.

"Yes," said Huey,
"when we come back
from the beach."

"We won't be long,"
said Louie.

"Well," said Grandma Duck, "they always find something else to do first. I guess I will have to load the truck myself."

And so she did.

Grandma drove her blue truck
to the mill.
The miller ground the grains
of wheat into flour.

When the miller
finished, he tipped
his hat and said
good-bye to Grandma.
"Good-bye," she said.

Then Grandma drove home with two sacks
of flour in the back of her blue truck.

When she reached the farm,
the boys were waiting for her.
    "Here we are," said Huey.
    "We're ready to help," said Louie.
    "How do we start?" asked Dewey.

"Hmm!" said Grandma. "You
are too late, as usual. I don't
need your help anymore."

"Now I am going
to bake myself a cake
with the flour from
my wheat," she said.

And she did.
She sifted the flour.

She mixed the batter.

Then she put the
batter in a cake
pan and put
the pan in
the oven.

The boys just
stood and watched.

Soon the cake
was done.
Grandma Duck
took it out
of the oven.
It smelled
so good!

"Wow!" said Huey.
"My favorite cake!"

"Don't bother
to frost it, Grandma,"
said Louie.

"We like it just the
way it is," said Dewey.

"Ha!" said Grandma Duck. "You did not help me plant the wheat. You did not help me cut it. You did not help me load the truck and take the wheat to the mill to be ground. I did without your help then. I can do without your help now. So run along." Then she took the frosted cake to the table.

The boys were very sad.
They went out and sat on the front steps.
They could still smell Grandma's
delicious cake.

"Grandma is right,"
said Louie.

"We didn't help,"
said Huey.

"Now we don't deserve
any cake," said Dewey.
"Let's tell her we are sorry."

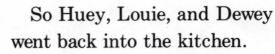

So Huey, Louie, and Dewey
went back into the kitchen.

"We're sorry, Grandma,"
they said. "We should have
helped you instead of always
doing what we wanted to do."

"Well," said Grandma
Duck, "I will forgive you
this time. But please
remember that we all have
to help one another."

Just then they heard
a car in the driveway.

They ran to the door.
It was Donald.
He was back from his long trip.
"Welcome back, Donald. We were
just going to have some cake."

They went inside and sat down
at the table.

Everyone had a great big piece
of Grandma's delicious cake.

When they had finished, Grandma asked,
"Now who is going to help with the dishes?"
"I will," said Huey.
"I will," said Louie.
"I will," said Dewey.

And they did.
Louie scrubbed
the pots and pans.

Dewey washed
the dishes
and glasses.

Huey wiped
the kitchen table.

"My, they are
good workers!"
said Donald.
Grandma just
smiled.

Soon it was time for Donald and the boys to go home.

Grandma waved good-bye.

"Come back soon," she said to Huey, Louie, and Dewey. "I am always happy to see good workers."

"We will," said Huey, Louie, and Dewey as they drove off with Uncle Donald.